PHERN H.

Copyright © 2021 by Phern H.

All rights reserved. No part of this book may be reproduced in any form or by any electronic or mechanical means, including information storage and retrieval systems, without permission in writing from the publisher, except by reviewers, who may quote brief passages in a review.

ISBN: 978-1-956736-73-1 (Paperback Edition)
ISBN: 978-1-956736-74-8 (Hardcover Edition)
ISBN: 978-1-956736-72-4 (E-book Edition)

Some characters and events in this book are fictitious. Any similarity to the real persons, living or dead, is coincidental and not intended by the author.

Book Ordering Information

Phone Number: 315 288-7939 ext. 1000 or 347-901-4920
Email: info@globalsummithouse.com
Global Summit House
www.globalsummithouse.com

Printed in the United States of America

Dedicated to:

People who have been forced to abandon their country because of beliefs that a person deserves human rights and treated with respect.

Advice

To contemporaneous migrants: there is nothing better than their own country, it does not matter what the struggles are.

Warning

If a person must move out from the own country be prepared for Discrimination, Racism, and Lack of opportunities of success. Smiles can be fake, soon they turn into mockery.

–Phern H.

NAIDAKAN, A DIFFERENT WORLD

Naidakan, a unique name for a country considered amongst the powers in the world is located in the Northern Hemisphere. Geographically extensive but relatively low in population. Historically recognized for its involvement in international politics as a mediator in belligerent conflicts; internally, is just another country that faces logical political conflicts that arguably, are indicators of popular democracy.

Latitudinal is divided into three zones: North, with extremely low temperatures that do not allow human survival. Even animal species seek refuge in caves in the winter season. The surface, covered with ice almost permanently, limits regular activities for the local economy; the heat that sunlight would produce is reduced by the temperature conditions in space and the frequent snowstorms that cover the surface for nearly half of the year. Aboriginal people located in this region dedicate their lives to hunting and fishing, The Central and South zones have temperatures that change four times throughout the year: Winter, which reaches temperatures up to 40 degrees below zero in the Celsius scale, with winds cooling the environment to 50 degrees; Spring, which is relatively rainy, helps in a low scale, the preparation of natural resources for a production of goods necessary for the survival of the inhabitants; Summer is relatively short, humid with an average temperature of 30 degrees. The cycle closes with Fall, temperature starts to fall down, but the final stage of outside productive activities reduces, the environment turns depressive but the ordinary activities of the social nuclei continue. The density of some zones is low, if related to the rest of the country.

Naidakan can also be observed in a longitudinal way; zones are West, Center, and East. The West and East are connected to oceans; they are rich in fishing and lumberyard. The center is rich in oil and natural gas. This condition generates the high concentration of population. The density of these areas makes a great deal of influence at election times.

Apparently, from early ages, the country was occupied by different groups. Immigrants from distant geographical areas where the systems of administration of a monarchical and imperial characters overwhelmed their inhabitants and subjected them to labor under the order of a power which caused hunger and misery among the villagers, forcing many survivors to escape to inhospitable regions; Poor people who in a nomadic style of life, were spread all over the old continent; merchants, as well as farmers whose lands had been expropriated by the victors in the battles; criminals, who in exchange for their freedom, took the risk of traveling into the unknown. Those were the first to invade Naidakan. They transplanted political mechanisms to take control of the territory, exterminated and removed the inhabitants from their lands, took illegal possession of the new world, showing disrespect and abuse towards people who owned the lands.

Trips to the new world continued throughout the years. All of them with the same goal: To exploit the resources. Survivors of the first adventures had circulated rumors about the wealth of the discovered lands; such comments gave place to sponsors to finance new journeys. Even the nobility was absorbed by the ambition for the new lands. The invasion continued. The phenomenon of immigration caused absolute changes in social, environmental, and geographical structures. Soon, the infrastructure became the fundamental inspirational motive of fighting, even between the immigrants themselves, whose ambition of controlling the economic resources of this geographical region, led them to kill each other. Invaders took with them different believes, thoughts and ideologies, naturals were displaced to remote areas where they lived in places known as reserves, receiving in return miserable sums of monetary resources that do not reached the minimum human of subsistence. Those subsidies came from a federal- style central government made up by immigrants.

The invaders tattered everything that represented an obstacle that could limit their ambitions. One of the steps towards achieving its objectives was the legalization of property. Of course with no opposition, everything was done in their own way. They completely ignored the existence of natural life and murdered those who opposed their goals. The elite began to manifest by itself and, with the help and support of the weapons they had manufactured, established their own methods of appropriation by enslaving those who, because of their human condition, used to work for survival. The invaders arranged the sharing of the lands, leaving out the aboriginals. The cultural values of the inhabitants were displaced. In a deliberately inhumane act, and in order not to be condemned by the other "civilized "countries, the new immigrants set up documents to legalize proprietorship of every place. Natives were forced to leave their lands, establishing that they would receive a financial fee and partial benefits, in compensation for the territories from which they had been displaced.

Aerial view of the North-East area of Naidakan

A COUNTRY IN DEVELOPMENT

Actually, the country has developed socially, economically, culturally and politically. The first governments regardless of the system, soon experienced the logical political deterioration over the years. But the seeds of ambition, corruption, discrimination, and abuse of power were already planted.

The new immigrants organized their ideals, doctrines, and beliefs. Different political groups emerged to participate in a leadership run, but all of them with similar goal: To administer the system to accumulate the benefits to themselves. Social preference for certain groups is quite discreet despite the existence of a document considered as the government guide, setting out the rights of the inhabitants. Leaders plead for equality among residents by all means, but the facts show the opposite. Practically, two main human forces make the social structure: The owner, the one who has the sources, and the worker. The first one makes up the rules; the second one obeys the rules. Immigration continues regularly. Cultural diversity is manifested in a variety of languages and moral values. It was given freedom of religion but Christianity by imposition controlled the largest percentage even though there were minor sects that differed by their rites and manifestations to pay tribute to different deities.

Current rulers reserve the right to admit new applicants, and enforce programs that benefit those from their similar background, ignoring the rest of the world. They forget or ignore the fact that they also are Descendant of immigrants. The requirements to get into this country are discretely manipulated to lead and protect the interests of the first immigrants. Eventually, an immigrant is selected from a poor country to cover international reputation, with logical consequences: deception, frustration, disappointment, and, logically, depression. The applicant professionalism is not recognized; new academically prepared immigrants arriving from those poor countries, are ignored and feel forced to work in low social status jobs. Professionals in the new Naidakan have their own organization which regulates who is able to practice a profession, that pushes the immigrant to restart an educative process by studies that result in exuberant and unattainable cost; there is also a group of immigrants admitted in an international political asylum agreement. These people have the choice of working immediately or improve the social status by attending educational institutions. If the immigrant is tenacious in his goals and meets the conditions that the system imposes, can apply for government-administered loans through the banking system to start studies; as a consequence the immigrant start his life in this country with a negative balance that is likely to remain for twenty years or more. Added that restarting studies means: age problems, family concerns, language barrier, as well as the self-discipline that the study requires. Then, as a graduated person at some age, finding a job is not any easy task. Although the legislation of this country states that no one can be denied a job opportunity for racism or discrimination, this principle is only part of the demagoguery; employers usually find an excuse to not hire the immigrant.

There are educational Institutions as the Universities which apparently allow access to as many applicants as they wish, but they have monetary quotas that only the privileged can afford without affecting their living status. This means that the doors to a profession are closed for a good part of the population. The limitation of the number of professionals is obvious and allows the monopoly of the services. Licenses or work permits in all areas are controlled by the same collegiate groups of professionals who establish the requirements to admit or reject new members as doctors, lawyers, engineers, architects, teachers, and all activities considered professional level.

Naidakan has his own way of administering justice. It is ridiculed by systems that disrespect the human condition. Leaders mock the general population when they send a citizen to prison for stealing minimal things in a commercial establishment but do not apply the law to those who from their position in power use government resources for personal purposes. A person who violently murders a human being is also sentenced to only five years in prison, and fifteen years are applied to those who do so by defending freedoms. The same group of leaders sets taxes and fees for small businesses working to survive, and monitors them constantly imposing sanctions when there is some slight mistake, but is consequent to large industrialists who violate wage laws and working conditions. There is a semi-autonomous institution whose operational role is to provide financial assistance to the worker while he is being unable to carry out normal duties, as well as to collaborate with the company in the expenses that the injured causes. Its financial resource consists of a government proportion and a percentage paid by companies, according to some conditions. Interestingly, when a small business finds it difficult to pay its dues, becomes subject of a legal article that allows the institution to recover the "debt" by expropriating the material resources that are in the company's name, and that the business requires for its operation, thus causing potential unemployment if the small company is forced to close doors or to acquire new debts that would impede community progress. When by special circumstances an employee becomes injured at work, the process to be followed would be very simple: the doctor determines the recovery time of the worker, depending on the severity of the situation, while determining the treatment to be applied; Once that time off is over, the worker is able to go back to work. The reality differs quite a bit in the process: the company, especially the large companies, require the worker as a productive force in the shortest possible time, for which the doctor changes his diagnostic and reduces the recovery time of the employee, attempting against the health of the worker. The Institution that should see for the interests of the worker, threatens to eliminate financial aid if the worker rejects the company's request. So the worker is forced to integrate into duties even if is physically disabled and unsuitable to perform duties. Leaders of the government show no interest in these cases, which obviously makes clear the protection to large businesses instead of protect the worker. If an employee dares to challenge any decision, the worker's identification is discreetly marked down and is subject of losing jobs, and chances of acquiring another opportunity become more difficult. Government works hard to show internationally a good reputation; propagate the idea that living in Naidakan is like finding a Paradise; enlarge numerically the natural wealth, stimulates international investment which the only beneficiary is the elite.

A PHYSICAL AND MENTALLY EXHAUSTED JOURNEY

The plane started to move. It was getting ready to take off from the airport, from the country where Amilkar's had been forced to leave. A country inhabited, in a high proportion, by a humble and perhaps naive population, people who used to fight for the rights when necessary. A land where many brains had fallen on a battlefront in an officially undeclared war which caused pain and sadness, especially in children and women who suffered the consequences. The ambition to take control of the wealth by the exploitative class, who used the natural and human resources for a private benefit, protected by a corrupt and obsolete military regime, had increased the poverty and misery among the population. Amilkar was leaving, beside his parents, friends, students and a few politicians he met, when he used to take the students to listen the debates of the congressmen. He didn't have political preference; neither intended to influence the students with ideologies; his teaching method was simple and transparent: to let the students to form their opinion of the legal, social and economic reality of the country. Thoughts like this had caused him threats in his life by paramilitary groups.

From his seat he looked at the landscape out there; closing his eyes he was trying to store that image in his brain; it seemed that everything he had done for his country was vanishing, like the clouds disappearing from his sight as the plane went on. With these thoughts he fell asleep.

The farewell had been very difficult. In the few relatives who went to say bye to him at the airport, he saw the entire population, the various communities where he had lived and had been forced to leave as security measures; he also remembered the student masses of various social strata for whom he had worked. Part of his life stayed with them. He knew that he would always exist in the memory of those who came to know him. At one point he thought to cancel his plane ticket and to send his family away so he would continue his job as usual by staying in the country facing the consequences, as the colonel threatened him. It was too late, the decision had been already taken.

He woke up when the pilot announced through the speakers that the plane was approaching to an airport. It was the first stop of the long trip. The passengers were asked to move to the waiting area where they would wait for the call to board another plane that would lead them to a different city. The waiting, which was scheduled for two hours, became martyrdom when it was announced that the flight had been delayed by eight hours due to mechanical damage to the aircraft. Amilkar's thoughts about what he left behind stayed fresh in his mind and showed no interest in knowing where he was temporarily. Travelers used to speak of the beautiful panorama offered by the city, but he claimed never been attracted by those luxuries. He used to see the poverty and humbleness of his people.

His family members were his wife, and four children. They waited anxiously and became restless as the time went on. One of the fellow travelers asked him for help to accompany him to find a place to buy some goodies. They proceeded to search for an establishment within the airport; when they had walked a few yards, they were intercepted by the airport security agents who questioned them about their intentions to leave the group. Those questions bothered him to the limit of feeling insulted, so he commented to the individuals that for him, that country was the least suitable to start a new life, a bellicose system by nature that invaded territories, unjustifiably murdering entire populations of innocents in the name of democracy, an etymologically manipulated word to numb the naive people; he was there forced by circumstances, but in his opinion, being there meant hell. The agents did not dare to challenge their interrogation and Amilkar and his friend returned to join the other passengers. They were eventually called to the window to move into the plane that would apparently take them to the new home.

The lack of familiarity with the steps to be followed in these circumstances, led him to consult with the employees before proceeding. They were assigned the seats on the plane. His youngest son, five years old, was placed in the front seat, next to him was a passenger who by his appearance could be an entrepreneur or someone similar. An ugly event happened when the child turned his head to consult his father: the passenger repressed him in an authoritarian voice that scared the child who became silent. It was the beginning of the cultural difference and discrimination's experiences. Of course the wake-up call by the man, was in a language totally unknown by his son, who had no idea what the passenger would have said to him, but the imperative tone scared him, so Amilkar asked the plane employee to help him exchange positions with his son. It was agreed and and he was placed next to the passenger who was continually looking at him; the passenger became uncomfortable and Amilkar asked him if his presence bothered him. The passenger simply kept quiet as Amilkar explained that the boy was only five years old and it was his first plane travel, so he was excited, and so being a little boy, his attitude was understandable. The passenger looked at him in a derogatory manner pretending to sleep for the rest of the trip. That passage was an indication of the future which was waiting for him.

They were eventually notified the approaching to an airport. The zone's s temperature was -37 degrees celsius; the snow was about two feet above the surface, the local television channels reported that the snowfall would continue over the next twenty-four Hours. The officer responsible for the group of immigrants asked them to wait until the rest of the passengers left the plane because Amilkar and his family had to visit a special office. It was 2:30 in the morning. When they finally left the plane, they were taken to an office designed to receive newcomers . He was tired and the airport officer who had been assigned to receive the documentation was temporarily absent. The employee checked the documents while another worker provided all newcomers, with coats, scarves, gloves, snow pants for the children, hats, and special shoes for walking in snow. Once changed clothes, the families were taken to a bus, which drove them to a hotel where they would rest. There, they were asked to order food. One of the fellow travelers who did not understand a slight word of the new language, asked him if he could order food for his six children. Of course Amilkar, accustomed to help people in need, got the satisfaction of being able to serve once again.

Although the place was considered a premium hotel, accommodation for him and his family consisted of a single room for six people. His wife and children fell asleep almost immediately; fatigue had dominated them. While his family was sleeping, Amilkar thought that the change he was experiencing was not significant enough for the sacrifice of leaving his country. The weather was not favorable, and he had already experienced signs of discrimination when he was on the plane. After a short break, Amilkar woke up his family, led them to the hotel's dining room, and ordered breakfast for everyone; when they were about to finish, he was called by a hotel's employee, to take the luggage as they might be driven back to the airport to board another plane that would drive them to another city. So they did it. They were the only passengers. Amilkar and his family boarded the bus which took them to the airport where they had arrived the night before, once there they walked into the plane to flight to where their place of residence would be. They would learn new customs, new social environment and perhaps a better life style, which for Amilkar meant nothing but a refuge or safe place for his family.

Weather condition in Naidakan when Amilkar arrived

The city where they had arrived was even colder than the other ones. The thermometer inside the airport marked minus thirty nine degrees. To Amilkar and his family surprise, this was not the end of the journey. It was late in the afternoon of the second day of non-break travel. There was another plane waiting for them. This was a small one. The flight would last about forty minutes. There was no option and they boarded the airplane which seemed to have a capacity to carry on about fifteen people. The passengers were just his family and two other persons. His kids talked to each other making comments of the temperature. As he watched the space: cloudy; the stars seemed to hide in his sight as if rejecting his presence. A few minutes later, lights began visible on what appeared to be the surface of the city. Everything was white as the foam of the sea that two days earlier he watched on the beaches of his country. He noticed a significant difference between the outlook he had left and the vision of the moment. The ocean foam he had left behind in his country was warm; instead, the whiteness of the snow was cold and static.

The small aircraft began to descend, the landing gear wheels sled down the runway, and he immediately felt a tremor in his body. It could not be explained whether it was because of the iciness of the landing place or the mixture of feelings and emotions of the moment. Once there: the unknown. Countless questions invaded his brain, all without an answer at the moment, but he would find the answer over time.

PROCESS OF ADAPTING TO THE NEW ENVIRONMENT

They left the small aircraft, submitted the necessary documentation and moved to a waiting room. It was early at evening at the airport of the city; a couple, apparently from the same origin of Amilkar, approached him, they identified themselves as workers for an office that used to welcome the new immigrants and helped them to establish, as well as to prepare the necessary papers for each visitor as a permanent resident. They were transferred to a hotel where they would stay while their future home was being prepared. The atmosphere was cold. The floor-to-ceiling windows in the room were completely covered in snow. They rested in two beds and eventually their family was able to sleep, for Amilkar it was a moment of meditation. Memories, friends, companions, the rest of the family and everything that was left behind, started to create images through his mind. There was no difference between day and night due to the cloudiness; the lights in the room remained on. On what would be his first day, after flying for two days almost consecutively.

He and his family were introduced with a person who identified as a government immigration officer. Amilkar got a warm welcome and was explained in a few words, the process of adaptation to follow once they were established. Immediately afterwards they were taken to the offices of the association that attended immigrants and were informed to the rights and obligations of the resident. Of course, at this point, they were instructed only about the obligations and situations that must be respected. He felt disrespected by the manner they were being treated. He was took as an ignorant who had asked for refuge, with academic level close to zero, however Amilkar would show them later, who he was and the type of professional they were dealing with. He was informed of the firmness of this country in terms of compliance with the laws. He was never mentioned about rights.

They spent three days in the little hotel. With no possibility to go out, it seemed to be a place of confinement. The radio and television reported on the temperature conditions and made suggestions that he understood little. There was an association responsible for enrolling school-age youth in school and at the appropriate level, as well as adults in a language teaching program that was considered a second language.

Three days after the arrival to the new city, the family was transferred to a house that would be the final destination. It was equipped with everything necessary to live comfortably. Amilkar avoided commenting that his emotions were far from the expected.

They had arrived to Naidakan, a country that for Amilkar, was only a temporary refuge, but for his family it meant the new home; their future, the rest of their life. Walking around the house, watching his children, he felt unable to plan or schedule future activities. He did not know in practice the society's usages; through the studies he learned about history and customs. Amilkar's concern was how to instruct his children when he did not know what this world had for him and his family. The low temperature kept them locked up in a jail without bars, that would not allow them to explore the outdoor.

The first weekend did not mean anything for him, it was just another day, but for the children it was totally different. The next day would be the first school day; a mixture of excitement and fear of the unknown. Amilkar felt useless. As a teacher, he knew that the first day of school is full of surprises for teachers and students. This time was different: new country, new language, and new environment. It was like sending them to face a world without having the resources to defend themselves. But he knew that his kids were smart enough to survive.

For minors, school registration was done prior to the arrival of the family. They were assigned the level of education, or grade, according to the corresponding ages; There were no options. Children started the educational process. Temperature conditions were not suitable for walking, but the lack of a means of transport forced them to do so. Amilkar was with them. He admired their courage. Among the barriers they faced in their educational process, the most difficult were: language, verbal insults and disdain from schoolmates. The youngest, with no school age, was scheduled to go to a special place where pseudo-educators used to take care of the kids. Amilkar never realized the sacrifice that this place meant to his son, who years later commented to him the treatment that kids received there. They used to be punished for different reasons, especially for language limitations, if they did not follow suggestions from workers. Shouting, pushing, insulting, were the most common actions. His son was to young and everyday meant for him the most inhuman way to deal with kids. He never commented it with his father for fear that he would justly complain to the authorities and this would generate retaliation against him. Amilkar felt like, in some way, his son was blaming him. His son was right. If his father knew about that situation, he would challenge the authorities of that institution to make sure that the responsible of such treatment towards kids, must had received the penalty they deserved. The program designed for immigrants as

Amilkar and his family, included a financial aid that would last until the adult was prepared in the language, and would be ready to join the workforce. The financial assistance also covered rent of the place of residence as well as as a budgetary amount for goods.

In that way he started a new phase of his life. In his mind, every day could mean the disappearance or extinction of his values. He felt in his skin the derogatory eyes and mocking manner from the people while visiting stores to make daily purchases; he experienced the Miserable and humiliating treatment by employees. There were few opportunities when he met honest people who showed him respect as a human been. It was like a total stranger in a new planet.

In the early days he received the visit of members of different religious sects and cultures, their purposes were to instruct him in the meaning of his dogmas. But when Amilkar identified himself with his values, many of them desisted in what they intended to instruct him. Several times he was offered help that seemed to be a condition to include him in group of followers. He never fell. He realized that this abundance of religious pastors, is an abuse of religious status in order not to pay taxes or to stay out of the workforce. Amilkar had solid moral principles and he refused to participate in dirty games. His answers were always oriented to human values. He had not come to Naidakan in search of God.

Amilkar began the process of learning the language in a hostile situation. With the exception of one instructor, the rest of them insisted that the survival activities of new immigrants were limited to the lowest level within the social strata. Most of the teaching resources were focused to learning a language that had been conditioned, strictly referring to the necessary communication to carry out low paid jobs, hence killing aspirations and immigrants' dreams, ignoring the professional readiness that some of them had, for a high level of performance; amongst the immigrants were school teachers, doctors, and accounting assistants, but that condition was ignored by the program. All were instructed in the same conventional and sometimes useless method. The program was more informative than instructional, planned to end after two periods in the same year. According to the government's plan, the immigrant would be prepared for the workforce after that period.

The discrimination of instructors towards immigrants, who had been sent to the city where Amilkar now resides was obvious. He never had the opportunity to select the zone or city in particular. The area's population was minimal, in proportion to the whole zone. Apparently the goal was to increase the population in that part of the country, with no human interest in helping the immigrant, who should help by working hard to the increase the wealth of the elite.

Months later, unexpectedly, Amilkar discovered through an article in the local newspaper that the person who ran the language instruction program for immigrants, as well as those who played the role of instructors, did not have the resources that an education teacher requires. That was the explanation of why the preparation of the language teaching program as a second language, lacked the didactic aspect; however, Amilkar's application, interest, cultural bases and basic knowledge of the language, led him to learn it easily and decided to embark on the search for a work, related to his academic level, which would allow him a modest income for his family group. With this goal in mind, he contacted the government office that was responsible to help immigrants to find a job. Soon, the first opportunity came. He got a phone call that woke up his spirit and enthusiasm. It was an employment interview offer. He prepared himself, and visited the place he had been informed, punctual and dressed up as he used to. At the first sight, the interviewer smiled at him in a sarcastic way, telling him that he did not need such clothes to clean desks or wash floors. He felt humiliated and left the place. However, he decided to show that he was not scared of a work, and accepted the challenge. Even though that he never did that before. He began a five-hour shift a day every afternoon. In the meantime, he volunteered at the school where his children were studying, helping teachers with students who had language problems.

In an opportunity a fellow teacher asked if he would like to try to work in the area of education. He replied that it would be a pleasure to have the opportunity to enter the education system. The teacher provided him with the name and address of a local private education center.

He showed up to the address that had been suggested. The first pleasant impression in the country was the familiar and respectful reception by the Principal. It was not an interview between a potential employer and a job candidate. It was a simple conversation as if they have known each other for many years. It was the first time, since he left his country, that he was received cordially in Naidakan. After a short talk, his new friend led him through the facilities of the center. The school had all the instruments to develop projects in the educational area. Amilkar sustained that the primary resources for a learning process are: interest, desire, and willness; the rest are instruments that can change according to the possibilities that society or responsible institutions have available, as well as a wise administration. His philosophy implies that the educational process requires vocationally prepared teachers. A project can be carried on in an opened-type school (no buildings). It can be taught and learned in public places, recreational parks, the cinema as an educational instrument, the church with integral moral values for society, without class preferences.

After the conversation, He was introduced by the principal to the other teachers as the new assistant of one of the higher grades. But not everything was brilliant. He felt in his skin the look of surprise of those who would be his work colleagues. In his attempt to differentiate them, he found curiosity, a few looked at him with respect, but for most of them Amilkar was just one more element in the school.

He was assigned a small room to be used to help students who for different reasons, were below average from the rest of the class. His first meeting with them was filled of surprises. After introduced himself to the few students, he was asked if he was coming from teaching at the jungle. Amilkar ignored the question and continued with the usual process of the individual introduction. A second student made a remark: he said that it was generally commented among the population, that those who came to the country from distant and poor places, were ignorant and they had arrived only in search of refuge. He also added that he heard from his parents that these individuals were only good for cleaning buildings, offices and restaurants. Amilkar commented that cultures have differences in various aspects and the reasons that move the individual to leave their place of origin must be respected. To the comment about the jungle, he responded to the group, that a teacher by vocation does not select the space where to educate and wherever is the necessity to learn by those at the jungle, there must be a teacher to satisfy that desire. Then he explained that cleaning is just a job, but if the immigrant is academically prepared, he should get a better opportunity, otherwise is another wasted brain. He also commented that he was new to the country and his knowledge of the system was not enough even to plan his activities from his position as teacher's assistant. In order to interact, he made an offer: at the same time that he helped them in their tasks, they would tell him about their origins. He established a friendly relationship that went unnoticed when he was with them, but years later.

He never felt comfortable. With the exception of two or three coworkers, the other teachers ignored his presence, or hypocritically addressed him including the new principal who was appointed a couple of years after Amilkar was hired. An arrogant and discriminative person. On several occasions and strategically, he had surprised those making comments out of all ethics, about him, even in front of some students.

After about four years of work, he experienced the worst of his dislikes at the school. While supervising the midday break, the bell announced the return to classes; Amilkar asked the students to orderly enter the classrooms; one of them, discipline problematic one, ignored the call in a rebellious manner he challenged the suggestion. This reaction was routine towards Amilkar, who had demonstrated serenity, patience, and professionalism to handle those situations; Amilkar called him to visit the principal's office. He was accused by the principal of threatening the student in a totally abusive manner, situation that was engineered by the same student. Amilkar did not try to defend himself, but in his conversation with the principal, he expressed his disappointment and told the teacher that the lack of professionalism of someone who pretend to be a teacher is easily perceivable, specially when trusting more to the malicious words of a student whose not exemplary behavior was known by all individuals at the school, than to a person who, like him, had shown that his only limitation was his new language. He also explained that a principal's duties go further more than occupying an office and a desk. At that point Amilkar submitted his resignation and, although the school year was not yet over, his decision had been already taken.

A NEW EPISODE IN AMILKAR'S LIFE

Amilkar had arrived to Naidakan. The living conditions of the city where he had arrived were different from those expected. Locating it on a map was easy, but meeting people and their Social structure was another task. Concerned about his future, he asked for an interview with an educational adviser from a high school; looking after the possibility to obtain equivalence for the studies he had done in his country of origin. It was reported that this process was almost impossible and he should not be able to receive even the equivalent of high school, so he would have to take high school subjects required to start studies at that institution. He recognized a certain deficiency while speaking the language, but did not admit academic deficiency. He felt ready to face any challenge and decided to start language studies, in a highly academic way.

Bad surprises never ended: he got a letter from the government asking him to return the money used in the travel from his country, including meals and clothing. He never signed a loan document but he didn't refuse to pay; Amilkar only asked for a reasonable time to pay back.

Amilkar decided to look for a job that would allow him to complete the expenses to support the family. Unfortunately the opportunities were less than nil. He submitted work applications to different companies. No positive answers. He had no choice but to challenge the High School principal suggestion and decided to apply at the local university which at his age meant many restrictions.

A few months earlier he had conducted a research on the conditions that the high education Centre required for regular students; he felt himself ready, so requested an interview with a student's counselors, it was granted almost immediately. He was given the application for registration as a student, including a student's loan application, in order to finance the studies. Both were accepted and he was admitted. The next step was to wait for the offer of studies that the university used to send to admitted students. Amilkar started the courses at the same time that he requested equivalence of the studies he had completed in his country of origin. It was initially reported that such assessment was worthless because they were in a language other than the local; in a new attempt, his request was admitted on the condition that he had to start taking classes, so his international assessment would be considered when received by the university authorities. He started in an environment made of young students, different language, and large groups. From the first participation in the group discussions he attracted the attention of the young classmates and teachers who looked at him with respect. Few immigrants from third world countries dared to start higher education. He was in his second year in humanities when he received the information that his equivalencies had been accepted by the university, that meant that Amilkar would not require to take all the subjects of the program, allowing him to graduate earlier than planned.

While studying, he applied for a job opportunity in one of the studies department of the university. The main requirement for this job was to write, read, and understand Amilkar's language. With no competition, he got the contract.

Taking classes while working, Amilkar spent almost two years, until the end of the project. Amilkar was sent to one of the most important meetings in the world, representing the sector for which he was lending his collaboration; his final report in both languages provided him with valuable marks toward his studies.

He also participated in another research. This was related to the area of his studies. It had to be performed on institutions that provided services for elders, places known as nursing homes; his work was focused on one of the most complicated areas in the human being: Seniors' behavior while living in a public or private institution. His research was conducted through direct interviews with the personnel, including nurses, nurse assistants, unit managers, and residents, amongst others. The results and report were also considered for final evaluation, and highly valued for the field.

Amilkar finished his studies and received the correspondent accreditation, without attending a protocol ceremony. His university degree was in the field of social sciences; he had chosen three areas which, in addition to being attracted to him, he had good bases for an excellent performance: Sociology, Psychology and Political Sciences. On one occasion he was asked for a reason why he was absent from the graduation ceremony, as this represents a dream for every student; he responded that his dream came true many years ago in his home country, when the greatest satisfaction of his life was fulfilled by receiving his diploma in Economic Sciences at the National University, as well as the high school teaching degree.

Although His life continued changing, the higher education in the new country had not taught him anything new, but a terminology in his new language. He considered that his academic level remained intact and the learning was due to his effort and not to the center of study. Amilkar's opinion is that the education system of Naidakan, automatizes students, so they are conditioned to a conservative social world, where political appearances change and the new professional is discreetly instructed to defend the interests of the power; wasting the advanced technological resources. That university purpose, unnoticed by students, keeps the community as a real puppet. It is said that the freedom of teaching is important, but a teacher is subject of suspension if comments disagree towards policies.

His job search continued in public education offices. After a series of interviews, he was hired as a teacher assistant to provide his services in the various elementary public education centers. His position was flexible and only if the institutions needed him, so his search for a stable position continued. He sent records of employment and personal references to different public and private institutions where a behavior manager or a health care support was sought. The answers were the same: experience was required. The institutions didn't count experience in another country, so it was difficult to acquire it, if not opportunity was given.

After about two years of search, he was hired by an agency which used to assist mentally and physically disabled people. He was assigned to a residence to work with three clients; their needs were completely different. Having a limited mental capacity, their attitudes needed to be oriented. One of them was easily irritable becoming aggressive and violent. The second person was friendly, cooperative, tolerant and submissive; these conditions make a person vulnerable to any kind of abuse and require a well-trained worker. Amilkar was confident in his knowledge and his first suggestion was to modify the criteria to accommodate clients; he also commented of homogeneity in the selection of individuals who would reside in the same place. His suggestions were ignored by supervisors, and he was advised to follow the agency's rules. His role was limited to prepare meals, to help clients with the laundry and household activities. Nothing related to his profession.

In various circumstances he witnessed verbal and physical assaults on workers by patients, the agencies ignored them. If the consequence was easily observable, the worker used to be blamed in order to cover apparent reputation.

The most significant aggression during his working time was the crime committed against a worker, by a patient, in one of the most prestigious institutions. Amilkar used to work with the person, so he understood the hostile and criminal inclination of such individual and had suggested the supervisor to select experienced workers to whom the task of supervising that person should be assigned. The agency ignored his suggestions, which possibly would have prevented the tragedy.

It took for him three and a half years to be hired by an agency where his experience and skills were considered. The individual's clinical history included violent actions toward his program's mates. Amilkar experienced his first challenge when the client refused to carry out his work duty and reacted aggressively against Amilkar, who professionally controlled the situation. From that moment on, the working environment became favorable for him. He was asked to participate in various recreation activities for the group, his peers approached him with working difficulties, which they did not express to the above levels of authority for fear of losing his job.

He was denied an opportunity to help his coworkers from a level with more authority, because the manager was scare of changes that Amilkar would make. However he continued his work as he had normally done. He did the same job for a long time, until he decided to request a temporary absence. It was granted: a month of mental rest. Amilkar used this time to meditate on the reality that surrounded him. He didn't see any good future. Returned to work with the same conditions. He started to feel mentally exhausted and decided to resign.

After a short medical treatment, Amilkar was ready to continue his working life. He applied for positions in which he could make decisions to modify certain elements of conduct management programs, which he considered none appropriate, but his views were never seen as a valid element, or were simply implemented as other's initiative. This bothered him enough to decide to silence his opinions.

Eventually he was hired by another agency with the same functions as the previous one. Nothing new came up, the same routine; agencies refused to change or modify behaviour programs.

Amilkar's suggestions implied to improve services, but he was not listened, he was an immigrant with no elite background. He started to feel the boredom of a routine. Programs were becoming obsolete and he felt useless, unable to help to make changes. That's how the years went by; getting older without having the opportunity he always waited for. He had reached the age to apply for retirement. Amilkar retired with a ridiculous pension, but he was mentally exhausted.

AMILKAR DECIDES TO OPEN HIS OWN AGENCY

It was an afternoon like others. He was thinking of how his life would be while in retirement. The routine at home was simple. He connected to the computer in search of opportunities to show that he was still in a position to serve the community, but when he thought about how he was treated by same society he had served, he felt humiliated. He had applied for his retirement, not only because he had reached the necessary age, but because of being denied the chances to escalate positions for which he was prepared, and given to others less qualified, but related to the boards' members. He had officially retired from his job in a rich country where the ridiculous pension he was receiving, was not even enough to pay a modicum rent in a decent place. Still, the pension system used to reduce the amount every year. A country of those which proclaim democracy and boast of being among the richest in the world, denying the acknowledgement of abandonment for a section of the population made up by the ones who gave their best years to build the country. Politicians in power who deny the existence of poverty, yet there are food banks that provide food to those in need. Leaders who lack the most valuable in humanity: Love for others. However, and without fear of reprisals, Amilkar used to write letters to the local newspaper to express his thoughts.

A few years before, he had planned his future, anticipating that his retirement would not meet basic needs. He commented to one of the few friends who used to be a member of the government parliament, his plan of retirement. The person suggested him the possibility of opening his own services' agency, given his academic preparation and skills,

After some consultations, Amilkar decided to carry on a project. The steps to follow on the operation took approximately two years: Research about the legality; conditions of the seniors' services marketing provided by other institutions; and his experiences from his previous works. He also consulted professionals in the mental health field, reviewed Healthcare magazines from organizations that were periodically published in the area of Psychology, Sociology, and medicine. He had a general knowledge acquired at the local university, as well as the one learned in his home country. Amongst his experiences he had learned that diseases and mental conditions have the same characteristics everywhere, but the treatments differ according to the professional human element, tools and instruments, and financial resources. These administrative elements work under the health care system, responsible for the application of medical procedures that benefit the population.

Once Amilkar had accomplished the first step, he was ready to prepare an operative plan. His Philosophy, defined the main purpose of the agency: To provide wellness to seniors and disabled individuals while being at home. He was trying to show that seniors at their houses can get better services, than being secluded in facilities, where they are exposed to abuses and misunderstandings. He also considered important the participation of the relatives, who, according to the legal agreement with the government authorities, and under different circumstances, may decide for the relative elders. His politics were focused on the personnel; the human element in healthcare institutions of this nature, despite the size of the organization, plays the most important role in the process. The direct worker must receive special attention, not only through an adequate salary, but with appreciation and esteem by recognizing that their efforts to provide happiness in the last years of the elders, is a virtue and a privilege.

Amilkar's agency was the only one designed as a private. No financial neither human resources were provided by the government health care administrators, although he had applied for them. His idea was competitive in some way. He did not want to fall into the usual problems like hiring employees for favoritism or nepotism, factors that allow the employee to commit abuses caused by lack of training and other virtues. His goal was to hire qualified personnel, according to the client's health condition, so everyone having the requirement, should have the opportunity to apply. Amilkar used to be an open minded person. The worker had the opportunity to express opinions; consulted decisions from supervisors eliminating a future possible complain, at the same time that help managers to take a more accurate decision.

A volunteer conducting a reunion with job applicants

He faced difficulties to enter into the healthcare market; it was not an easy task; there were state-protected monsters with years of operation which used traditional system based on Government subsidies. Its social members used to participate in associations giving the appearance to have a philanthropic dedication, making it public by using newspapers and arranged interviews published in health-related pamphlets and magazines. In fact, their role was limited to social exhibitionism.

Amilkar had a strong confidence on his project. The lack of financial element did not stop him. Some loan rejections from financial institutions moved him to operate the agency with his personal resources. The agency met the legal requirements and it was registered. Amilkar visited the healthcare department which was responsible to approve financial help to persons in need, his plan was to offer the agency as an option as a service provider. He felt disappointed. He was notified that, according to the agreement of the administrators of existing agencies, a new service provider would not be allowed to serve incapacitated individuals "until new order". The monopolization was obvious, even though the existing institutions had made public no having spaces for new applicants. However, he proceeded to prepare pamphlets giving complete information of the services provided by the new agency. He personally distributed them around the city. Asked the local newspaper for a minimum space, he was granted a phone interview which was published in a routine edition.

Amilkar began another stage of his life in a country that did not prove to be as minimal as the outside world knows. He was not prepared to face the battle against the big rivals; not large in quality but supported by their history and the social apparatus; institutions involved in the healthcare system, which in a discreet way, used to support them financially, even by preferentially sending people who required the services that Amilkar provided. Those agencies also had the use of the media available to spread the few virtues they had but hiding internal corruption. The management members used to be named because their familiarity with the political parties on duty, but many of them were completely ignorant of the healthcare area. He was facing a well-known field, where he had worked for several institutions. In all of them he was recognized as a fighter for workers' rights. His co-worker were silent about the abuse and mistreatment of supervisors and administrators for fear of being fired. Amilkar did not fear Reprisals and openly expressed his opinion when he felt that circumstances did not favor the employee. However it was a vain struggle. Most of the co-workers, accustomed to a "yes" routine to everything that was happening, did not understand the difference in their activities, whether they were in the job description or not, and they were being abused. He was trying to teach the employers the human side of an employee.

A few months after the pamphlets distribution, Amilkar got the first opportunity to serve. The person was in a nearby town; after the legal arrangement, he started the job by himself. The contract was for a short period but it was good for Amilkar.. It was his first experience as a business manager. Eventually, a new potential client approached him, looking for health care services for a family member whose behavior was aggressive due to his mental impairment. This was the specific field of Amilkar. He took the contract, and started a simple but effective treatment. After a reasonable period, the family members started to observe positive results and decided to continue with Amilkar's services. The agency's reputation had already begun.

Volunteer providing information about the services

The requests for information about the agency services increased and Amilkar had to hire personnel. He decided to use the local newspaper to look for employees; after the first publication, he received an unexpected number of local applicants who, after an interview and being explained their role, decided not to take the offer. With some exceptions, local workers did not show interest in the healthcare area even though many of them had credentials. Nevertheless, Amilkar continued booking interviews with some applicants, at meantime more clients approached him seeking for services. He hired the first workers under his supervision. At the senior's request, Amilkar used to take charge of the job himself, providing at the same time, training to the other employees. It was necessary to keep the good reputation among clients and employees from other agencies.

Amilkar was contacted by a person who used to process contracts with foreign workers who were interested to work in the healthcare area. His concern was the licit manner to contract them. With no obstacles, the first workers started to arrive to Naidakan. All of them had a job contract with Amilkar's agency. They demonstrated a high level of professionalism and ethics, even though their documentation was not legally recognized, they were authorized to work. The clients were happy with the services and soon they became the references to advertise the Amilkar's agency services. They had experience in the senior's services area and the qualifications that the healthcare department required. Amilkar was trying to show the government the appropriate method to attract people from other cultures.

The first two years did not fill up Amilkar's expectations; they meant financial misfortune. His principle was that seniors and employees are first, profit comes later.

Amilkar did some analysis which led to some changes to continue his endeavor. The finances increased to the extent that Amilkar finally had the opportunity to take a vacation. Five years of hard work deserved to be celebrated with all the members of the staff, it was no difference between supervisor, manager or direct worker. It was a single family which had fulfilled obligations, and accomplished the main goal: Seniors satisfaction.

Workers who had been with Amilkar since their arrival to the country.

Amilkar had been invited before, by one of the worker's family, to visit their country. It would be a new experience that he accepted, an adventure into another unknown country. Culturally, he had become familiar with the professional and ethical attitude of those who worked with him. But he wanted to distance himself for a while from the physical and mental demands that his work required.

As a visitor it is not easy to say that the adaptation process will come later. Live the moment as it currently is. His employee family showed a special interest in his visit. Among the objectives that guided him to carry out this adventure was to get familiar with some healthcare topics related with his agency. A couple of months after the celebration he left to the new country where he found warmth, energy and cordiality of people. His mind brought him memories of his country of origin; the humility and courtesy of the inhabitants reminded him his cultural roots. He was welcomed by the family who invited him.

Amilkar used to live in a country whose internal social and cultural values differ from the ones made public abroad. In conversations with other residents, they themselves admit to live in a society full of envy and selfishness. In this adventure he was having the real treatment as human being.

He found out that the quality of professionals was at the same level as others from developed countries, but the economic constraint does not allow them to have the material resources as high technology. The population had a human quality and understanding; these values allow them to live together without a social competition problem. The religious aspect is notorious and respected by all. Amilkar lived within religion but without denomination. He sustains that the individual who has the possibility of helping and refuses to do so, is against the human species, failing in the moral character. He visited places whose nature made him forget the problems caused by the society in which he resided. Churches, parks, popular markets, museums; everything seemed like he was going back to his childhood, to his youthful years. On one occasion he was asked by a young woman who knew him by references, whether there is a certain moment when the person experiences the emergence of maturity. His answer: When a person, having the appropriate orientation, feels ready to differentiate the right and wrong from his attitudes, this leads the individual to choose the best option; the satisfaction of a mission accomplished and the anxiety to learn are positive signs, but remorse and discomfort are signs of failure. He saw students at schools wearing uniforms that differentiated them from institution to institution, in a disciplined manner; the colorful streets, the joy of being involved in the educational process. His years as a teacher in his country were present in his mind.

View of the visiting country

Unfortunately, peace and tranquility had an end. Many times he had wondered why misfortunes caused by humanity, last longer than good works.

His journey was over and he had to return to the mud. He said goodbye to people who showed him that somewhere in the world, he was estimated in his values.

AWAKENING OF A DREAM

His trip back to Naidakan was exhaustive. Some news were waiting for him at his office. Some years before, Amilkar had submitted to the corresponding office, the tax documents demanded by the government every end of year. To his surprise, a few months later, when the legal time to file such records had ended, he was informed by the same office that the agency didn't submit the government documents and he had been financially penalized. Immediately he contacted the responsible office to make clear that he, personally filled out the documents and sent them by regular mail.

Professionalism and skilled workers were requirements to work at Amilkar's agency

He was communicated in a non-professional manner that the government's office was no responsible for any company's problems. Amilkar didn't argue and submitted the documents again.

Confident that this time there would be no problem, he told his employees that everything was settled down. After a reasonable time he decided to consult the tax office. The response he received amazed him. Again, the office had no reference to any of the documents. No one at the government's office admitted to be responsible and Amilkar was suggested to send them again. He had no choice given the irresponsibility of public employees. He prepared the shipment again; this time he did it simultaneously through the computer system, with a government employee. It was the only way to ensure that the documents were received by the office. Unfortunately the bad news didn't end up there. Upon receiving the state of accounts from the government, it included the two packages of documents that had not apparently been received, plus the third one, accumulating a considerable sum beyond Amilkar's reach. No one in the tax office was held responsible. Amilkar refused to make any payment until the situation was clear. He also asked for an official apology as well as admit their mistake. The apology never was received and the corresponding numbers were not corrected. Considering that the law and reason were on his side, he decided to file for bankruptcy. This step would allow him to restart a project but also limit his credit possibilities.

As long as the tax offices continued the tax task of destroying the Amilkar project, the government office ordered an audit that was apparently carried out by randomly selecting the companies that would be the subject of that annual review. The first year was justified, he had just solved his first difficulty and the tax department was not satisfied with it, even though their pride did not allow them to admit that everything was caused by their irresponsibility. The operation was carried out; the findings were minimal and solvable differences. The next year, and also randomly, Amilkar's small business was selected for another audit, again without any negative results. However, it was not done yet to him. No doubt that he became the focus of some conspiracy by competitors or the government by itself. His performance in the seniors market had opened the curiosity from other agencies. He was making clear the corruption in healthcare services and for the third consecutive year, he was selected for another audit. this time with a single variant: its account number to report deductions from the schedule payments to employees had been changed. Amilkar was in trouble. The tax office had found a way to destroy his project. The battle with the giant of the world started; he had been assigned a new number without having received a letter or at least a brief note. It was reported that it was his responsibility to consult for the change. A few years earlier, a friend had told him, in a very discreet manner that the employees of the country's tax office hold all the power in their hands and consider themselves infallible. He was experiencing this reality. They did not understand reasons and despite the mistakes made, they did not feel responsible for them; they were always looking for somebody to pay for their mistakes. Amilkar wondered if their attitude was the same with the great politicians and business moguls.

Despite all the difficulties he continued with his plan, while preparing a new trip abroad. On this occasion his goal was to search possibilities to collaborate in some way, with the development of the community where he planned to stay for a long time. He didn't think about making money, not because he didn't need financial income, which of course is always well received, but because of the anxiety of continuing the education process in which he had vast experience. Helping those who require help in the psychological process is humanity's responsibility, he said. The behaviors and attitudes of the individuals need to be modeled from the moment of spawn. Society is responsible for preparing the environment so that the individual does not become an isolated person and vulnerable to get into the conflictive society.

With this second adventure he intended to momentarily distance himself from the difficult circumstances before, simply because the negligence of certain government employees.

He prepared the necessary documentation, instructed the person who would be at the head of the institution in his absence. He felt mentally exhausted by all the incidents that had recently affected not only his reputation, but also the insecurity of continuing his project. He thought about the confidence that his friends had in him. Amilkar was scared to fail them.

This time he was thinking in a new experiment. His goal was to search the seniors market in that small and poor country. A long trip, twenty-three hours of flying time. The movement at the airports, the endless wait in the corridors, unknown people who walked fast in order not to miss their flights, and others like Amilkar, trying to kill the time in a semi-dormant way on the waiting benches; it was the routine at the airports. After about two days he arrives at the destination. A different city from the previous one. Quite in appearance but with more commercial activity. The constant coming and going of people; he could feel the cultural warmth that this society offered him, unlike that the one received in the country of his residence. He stayed in a studio apartment that had been booked a few days before his arrival, by a family he had met on his previous trip. That place would be the headquarters to continue his job. He had been greeted with the kindness that a family group uses towards a true friend. Amilkar planned to know more about local usages: he was invited to attend a funeral of a prominent member of the local authorities. As part of the ceremonial, he participated in a meal after the normal ritual of a burial. He was invited to visit the local museum, colonial-style churches.

A local girl in a peaceful like position at a white sand beach

Amilkar also tried a boat trip by the shores. The panorama was a paradise, islands everywhere, a white sandy beach that invited to forget the obstacles that life presented to him in his country of residence; the heat by a bright sun was reduced by the coconut tree palms, sending a cool ocean breeze. The arrival back to the land was not a pleasant one, a little accident happened and Amilkar was taken to the hospital. The incident gave to Amilkar an opportunity that he longed for: to know the government's hospital services in a provincial community, as they call the far- flung places of the city. He was taken care immediately, without any protocol. He observed the diligence of nurses and workers who, by their gestures led the message of give him preferential attention because he was a visitor, Amilkar refused to get that status; he told them that he was no one special and they could perform a normal use as with someone else. Of course to make that comment used his friends because he did not speak their language.

The doctor attended and fixed the situation temporarily, until it was treated in another hospital by a specialist where he talked with doctors and nurses; he was trying to learn more about the healthcare system. His journey ended not with a good foot literally, but he could not delay his trip.

Another chapter of his life was to end. Amilkar returned to his apartment. The departure time approached fast. He had a few more days; then the farewell. He was restless because his foot was still in poor condition. Again his spirit felt down. He was reluctant to return to a hostile medium, filled up by envy, discrimination, materialist in the wrong interpretation. He was taken to the airport, boarded the plane. Another long nightmare trip. Finally the plane approached to its destination. He felt anguish, fear and resentment. Another world was waiting for him.

Back to his county, he rested for a few days before going back to the office.

Amilkar had put forward solutions that would easier the end of the agony. He made proposals to the government office with no answer. Hired a lawyer to take charge of his case and after some time he was informed that fighting against the government was a non-sense action. Time passed and he felt abandoned physically and morally exhausted; only the trust of his employees reassured him. After a reasonable time he decided to terminate the operations of his small agency services. The monster had defeated him; he was experiencing the same as Other small companies which did not belong to the elite and had been forced to close their doors. The system was not interested in the well- being of employees who would lose their jobs, neither of the senior's population; its only goal was money produced by labor force, which would allow it to demonstrate to the world a false democracy and a dubious moral reputation.

There are many new immigrants in this country, who, like Amilkar, were forced to leave their country, they arrive believing in the honesty of Naidakan's leaders; they immigrated there, with dreams, illusions and plans for a better life; instead they find a modern enslaved system, which uses a demagogic and insulting language for other countries having a different political system; Naidakan engages in military actions against poor nations, killing children and innocent people, in the name of the democracy. Arrogant alliance with other big nation, manage the world towards hatred, discrimination and racism. Send ridiculous help to the poor countries, only to cover reputation.

Of course, there are groups of new immigrants who refuse to accept that the modern slavery is real, and surrender their moral values. They feel ashamed to express their opinion, or simply they fear retaliation from the Naidakan system.

It is currently unknown what became of Amilkar Alvarenga. His employees remember him with respect and admiration. A man who was discreetly pushed to leave his country for clearly expressing the abuses of the imperialist sector against the honest worker, to fall into the hands of another which only difference is its territorial quantity, but morally is sunk in the corruption where the abuses are discreetly erased in front of the international community, creating a false reputation for kindness and prestige.

www.ingramcontent.com/pod-product-compliance
Lightning Source LLC
LaVergne TN
LVHW040202080526
838202LV00042B/3288